D1456317

SECRETS

Also Available by Dr. Barbara Becker Holstein:

The Truth: Diary of a Gutsy Tween

SECRETS

Diary of a Gutsy Teen

DR. BARBARA BECKER HOLSTEIN

Sky Pony Press
New York

Sky Pony Press books may be purchased in bulk at special discounts for sales promotion, corporate gifts, fund-raising, or educational purposes. Special editions can also be created to specifications. For details, contact the Special Sales Department, Sky Pony Press, 307 West 36th Street, 11th Floor, New York, NY 10018 or info@skyhorsepublishing.com.

Sky Pony® is a registered trademark of Skyhorse Publishing, Inc.®, a Delaware corporation.

Visit our website at www.skyponypress.com.

10 9 8 7 6 5 4 3 2 1

Manufactured in China, November 2014
This product conforms to CPSIA 2008

Library of Congress Cataloging-in-Publication Data

Holstein, Barbara Becker.
Secrets: diary of a gutsy teen/Dr. Barbara Becker Holstein.
pages cm
Summary: "From new school experience to a new baby in the family to a new crush, this new teen finally feels empowered on making her own decisions with confidence and keeping those secrets she holds dearest for herself"—Provided by publisher.
ISBN 978-1-62914-626-3 (hc: alk. paper)
[1. Growth—Fiction. 2. Emotions—Fiction. 3. Self-perception—Fiction. 4. Friendship—Fiction. 5. Secrets—Fiction. 6. Diaries—Fiction.] I. Title.
PZ7.H73877Se 2015
[Fic]—dc23
2014036824

Cover design by Victoria Bellavia

Interior design by Sara Kitchen
Interior illustrations by Julie Matysik

Ebook ISBN: 978-1-63220-225-3

INTRODUCTION

One day I decided to find a way to combine what I already knew as a girl with the knowledge I have as a psychologist. That decision led to a girl coming to life as the main character in the first book in this series: *The Truth: Diary of a Gusty Tween*. The girl kept a diary and had a lot to say. She knew a lot about important things that many adults brush aside or forget. Many readers told me that they identified with things that happened to the girl. Readers related to her honesty and to how real she was. Many shared her awareness of the truth.

As *The Truth* ends, the girl's life is changing drastically: she is moving to a new town, her mom is having a baby, and her crush on Paul is just about over. She has solved a mystery and has developed a secret way to hold onto the best of herself as she grows up.

In *Secrets: Diary of a Gutsy Teen*, the girl is back with lots more to share in her diary—a new school, a new baby in the family, new friends; everything has changed for her. There is a new crush about to happen and lots of adventures. There are new best friends and some unsettling social dilemmas. Some of these dilemmas involve boys. There are secrets to share and secrets to keep to herself. There are problems to solve and . . .

But I had better get out of the girl's way. She really wants to begin.

SECRETS

Diary of a Gutsy Teen

This is my secret diary. Not the one that says "My Special Diary." I leave that around just to fool grown-ups. This is the <u>real</u> truth. This is where I will write all of my secrets that I don't want to share with anyone but you!

Dear Diary,

 I can't believe it. Today we moved, and I feel like I'm in a dream. I just keep walking around our new house and wondering when we will go home. It feels so different and strange. Everything is on one floor (that's called a ranch house). The floors are all bare wood. My mom said our rugs would look terrible here so she let the people who bought our old house keep them. I think she was probably right. They were a dark maroon and the walls here are a light cream. I don't think that would look good.

 I went to the bathroom three times since we got here and every time I used a different bathroom. I can't believe it. Three different toilets in the same house! Only my friend Susan, my rich friend, had more than two bathrooms in her house. And four bedrooms! And a family room. I can't believe we have this much space now.

 When I look out of the windows I expect to see the shrubs and the Hudson's house which was next to us on the left, but I don't. Instead, I see a big open field that will probably have houses built on it by next year. That's what my dad said anyway. And when I look out to the right I expect to see our clothesline and the Dixon's driveway, but instead I see rose bushes and a wooden bench under a tree that the last owners said we could have.

Tonight, we had to eat supper off paper plates and use plastic forks, knives, and spoons because our boxes are still packed. My aunt made us a big picnic basket full of food and that's what we ate for supper. It was delicious. There was fried chicken, potato salad and potato chips, cupcakes for dessert, and fruit salad. And at the bottom of the basket under the ice was a whole package of Hershey Kisses. Yum!

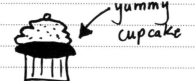

My brother already started to play with a kid next door who's about a year older than he is. He's so lucky. I have no new friends yet and that's the truth!

Dear Diary,

I feel so lonely. I can't believe my parents made us move. Don't they understand how awful it is for me? I don't have anyone to share secrets with. I talk to Angela on the phone, but it isn't the same. Sometimes when I'm on the phone with her I get the feeling that she is on her computer at the same time or maybe just thinking about other stuff. I don't feel that closeness with her anymore. I want to feel it, but I don't know how. I'm afraid to ask her if she is playing a game on the computer or chatting on Facebook at the same time as she's on the phone with me.

The only good thing that happened is I asked Angela if she wants to send selfies back and forth to each other. My phone is old and I don't have FaceTime, but I can still take pictures and send them to her. She loved the idea, so I spent hours yesterday sending her pictures of me in different rooms in my house and in the backyard, too. It was a lot of fun. I dressed up as if I was putting on a play and each room was a new scene. I wore a velvet scarf and one of my mom's fancy hats and put on an old long petticoat I used to dress up in as a kid and then I went outside and stood on the swing that is hanging from a tree. It was hard to keep the swing still enough to get a good selfie, but finally I did, and I sent it to Angela.

She sent back a selfie of herself dressed up like a Flapper girl from the 1920s, posing with a long stick as if it was a cigarette in a holder.

We laughed and laughed on the phone, and it was the best I have felt since we moved. The best part was that if felt like we were together again even though we are apart!

Dear Diary,

I miss everyone and everything. Of course I miss Paul, even though I was feeling my love for him could never really last. I even miss Debbie down the street who I really hated. I'm so lonely. I feel like my whole world was taken away from me when we moved here. Everyone else in my family seems so happy. My mom is singing all the time—even though she throws up sometimes in the morning from being pregnant—and my dad keeps saying how glad he is that he took this new job and how successful he's going to be. My brother is out the door and playing with Johnny (the neighbor boy) as soon as he's allowed to in the morning. And here I am, stuck inside. I am miserable.

I cried and cried last night into my pillow. No one heard me—at least if they did, they didn't come asking what was wrong. When I fell asleep I dreamed that we had moved back to Springport and everything was just the same as it always was. In my dream Paul had grown about six inches, and I was so happy.

When I woke up this morning, I was sad again.

I've been unpacking for days but I still can't find a lot of my special things. At least I have my locket. I wore it in the car when we moved here so I wouldn't lose it. Every night I put it on the night table next to my bed. I guess when I get a poodle dog I'll have to put it away more safely so she doesn't accidentally eat it. And when the baby is born I'll also have to be careful. Angela has a little sister and she ripped and ruined so many of her things it was terrible. If the baby destroys any of my things I'll hate that baby forever.

Dear Diary,

    I can't find some of my favorite stuffed animals anywhere! I can't find my stuffed toy poodle dog—the one that I've had since I was a baby. Fifi, where are you? I need to cuddle you. I'm too old to cuddle my baby dolls and they're in a box in the back of the closet, but I could really use a good snuggle with Fifi right about now. I also can't find five of my favorite Nancy Drew books or the cards that the kids in my class gave me the last day of school when they wished me well. I wonder if the movers left that one special box at our old house. I hope not!

Dear Diary,

My mom just told me that the baby is a girl. I don't know how I feel. On the one hand, I like the idea of a cute baby girl that I can dress up and put bows in her hair. On the other hand, I feel jealous. My parents already have a daughter—that's me! Why do they need another one? Aren't I good enough? What if she is prettier or smarter than I am? What if they like to be with her more than they do with me? I know we are going to be many years apart in age, but still I don't like having these bad feelings. I wish she was a boy. My brother wouldn't care. You know how he doesn't care about anything as long as he gets to play and watch TV. His mind is so much easier to be inside of than mine. He is just as happy living here as in Springport. Of course he is so much younger than I am, too. Maybe things that bother me will bother him when he gets older.

The only good news is that I found all my stuff. There was an extra box still left in the back of the garage. Fifi is back on my bed, ready to be hugged and cuddled when I get into bed tonight. I'm still hoping that I will have a real dog soon! Does anyone out there in the universe hear me? I need a dog that is alive. I need new friends. I need a life!

Dear Diary,

My dad set up the computer, finally! I hope it doesn't crash any time soon since it's still pretty old. Me, Angela, Betty, and all my friends spent hours on Facebook writing back and forth to each other and posting selfies. It was such fun. We decided that we are going to have a task to do every day and send a picture to each other after completing it. Tomorrow we are each going to cook something and then post a picture of what we cook. I'm going to make spaghetti and sauce with sliced mushrooms. My mom helped me think of what to make that wasn't too hard and we already have all the ingredients in the house. Then the day after tomorrow everyone has to take a picture of something interesting outside that we see and post it. I don't know what to take yet. But it is fun to still be connected with my old friends this way, and I'll figure something interesting to post. I guess when school starts we might be too busy to continue every day. But for now, it gives me something to look forward to when I wake up.

Dear Diary,

We have another week before school starts. I'm scared about going to a new school and not having any friends and never having anyone to talk to or laugh with. Can you believe that my brother already has three kids on this block to play with and I have no one? I miss Angela so much, and I'm jealous that she's hanging out with other kids. Maybe they are sharing secrets like she and I once did. Maybe she already has a new best friend? I'm so alone.

I'm also scared that the homework will be really hard and I won't like school. I'm scared that no one in my class will like me. I'm scared that I'm never going to feel like myself again and that's the truth.

Dear Diary,

　　Dad took us all to the movies tonight. He said we had to get out and get used to our new town. He drove us downtown and we parked near the movie theater. The downtown is pretty. There's one small department store, named Epstein's. It's only about one fourth the size of the department store we had in Springport. There's a big public library that looks nice and a lot of small boutique stores. I kind of like the downtown, actually. And the bus goes there from the end of our street, so I'll be able to go downtown by myself, just like I did in my old town.

　　We saw a great movie. It was a comedy and it was really funny. This guy said a lot of silly things all the time and got himself in trouble. At the end of the story he suddenly says everything right and becomes rich and everybody stops making fun of him. I liked the ending.

　　I felt good tonight, except for my brother kicking me in the leg all the time when we were at the movies. He doesn't realize that he keeps doing it. I have to try to push his leg over so he doesn't kick me, but it never works. He gets so excited watching movies that he forgets and kicks his legs. No one was sitting on his other side, thankfully. Now I have a big nasty looking bruise on my leg.

But at least I felt normal tonight. It was like in the past when we did things together as a family more often.

A few more days and then school starts. I'll be in eighth grade. I'm really nervous still.

I hope my new school is good. I have never been so scared in all my life and that's the truth.

Dear Diary,

Today, Dad took me to school on his way to work. I got up early and took a shower. I even used the deodorant that my mom bought me this summer. I felt funny rolling it on under my arms. But I have to do it: I don't want to smell under my arms, especially not on my first day at a new school!

I put on my new outfit—the one Mom bought for me last week when we went shopping. It's a shirtdress with black leggings. I also put on my new Chucks. Then we had breakfast. Mom made French toast as a first-day-of-school treat. I couldn't eat much, though. My stomach felt like it had rocks in it.

Then Dad drove me to the middle school. In Springport I would have been in the same building up to the eighth grade but here they have a separate building for seventh, eighth, and ninth grades. The building is dark red brick and very big. It has three floors.

My legs were trembling when we walked inside to the principal's office. I was sweating and could feel my heart racing. The halls were full of kids, and I didn't know anyone! The older kids looked gigantic. The boys were so tall, like grown-ups. The girls had makeup on. Lots of it. I couldn't help staring at them.

The day flew by. I was glad that a nice girl, Betty Ann, came up to me and showed me around. I was also glad I had used lots of deodorant because I kept sweating all day. I was so nervous. To calm myself I rubbed my locket—you know, the one with my secret message to myself in it that Aunt Belinda gave me for my birthday two years ago. That helped make me feel a little less nervous.

Betty Ann is pretty. She has dark brown eyes and reddish brown hair almost down to her waist. I love long hair and wish mine was as long as Betty Ann's.

Betty Ann was so nice to me all day, never leaving my side. We go to a different room for science and another for social studies but all the other classes are in our homeroom with Miss Brown. Oh, we also go to the big kitchen room for our home economics class. We're going to make chocolate cake tomorrow. I'm so excited! I love to cook!

There's a lunchroom in the basement of the building and that's where we have lunch. Betty

Ann sat with me and some of the other girls in our homeroom class sat with us, too. Their names are Sally, Judy, and Joanne.

The food was awful. It was all greasy and not hot enough. And the whole lunchroom smelled gross. I almost felt like I would throw up and I'm not even having a baby. But I didn't. Tomorrow I'm going to make a tuna fish sandwich and bring it in a brown bag like Betty Ann does.

Betty Ann gave me her phone number and email address and I gave her mine. She called me tonight and we talked for a long time until my dad told me to go to sleep. I checked my email before going to bed and already had an email from Betty Ann saying that she'll see me tomorrow.

I'm so happy that Betty Ann likes me. I think I might be happy in my new school and new home. Maybe that's the truth. I hope so.

Dear Diary,

I'm not so sure that some of the other girls in my class like me. Betty Ann is fun to be around, but I'm beginning to realize that she is not so popular. Maybe it's because she is smart and a little nerdy. I like smart girls, but I can see that some of the other girls kind of ignore her. They are always sending notes to each other and laughing together in the hall, and Betty Ann isn't part of their groups. Now that I'm with Betty Ann a lot, the girls don't talk to me, either. I might have been imagining this, but I thought that Sally walked away from me as I came near to her in the hall yesterday. I felt really weird.

We were all friends in my old school. Angela was my best friend, but I was friends with everyone, except Betsy who was mean to me a few times. I wasn't expecting all the girls to have cliques here. Now I have only one friend and because of her I might not have too many others. I still hate it here! I wish I were old enough to get on a bus and go back to my old school and just live at Angela's house.

Dear Diary,

Angela sent me a selfie of all of my old friends hanging out after school on the soccer field behind the school. They were all waving to me and holding a sign that read WE MISS YOU. I felt so sad seeing it. Mom promised to take me to visit Angela in a few weeks, but she is getting so gigantic and has trouble with her feet swelling because of the baby that I wonder if she will really take me. Maybe Grandma can drive me. I'm going to call her and find out. I need to see my friends. The hole in my heart is getting bigger and bigger. They are now the most important people in the world to me. I feel like everything I think and want to share just feels empty and no fun without them to share it with. I hate this house. I hate my family. I hate this move. Help! Somebody help!

I wrote this poem last night:

hole

Who is there to care about me?
Who sees what I see?
Who can help me through the
darkness of day and night?
Who cares enough to share my plight?
Tell me when all this will end?
Tell me when I will feel good again.

Dear Diary,

I cried for three hours in my bed last night before I fell asleep. I realized that I'll never be a child again. It's over. It's finished. I can't believe it. I'll never be able just play with my dolls and read books for hours. I'll never have armpits with no hair under them ever again. And any day now I'll probably get my period. My mom told me that she got hers when she was twelve, so I'm way overdue.

I'm so miserable. How could anyone ever want to grow up? I can't believe I have to leave so much behind. And I don't know what's coming. I just know I'll have more and more homework and less and less time to just be myself. And on top of it I will have to help my mom with a new baby soon. I'm miserable. I want to be nine again and just play outside after school and ride my bike without having to worry about school and friends and getting my period.

Dear Diary,

My parents told me last week that I was getting a surprise soon, since we couldn't really celebrate my birthday last spring because we were packing to move. Today was the day! My mom and dad woke me up early this morning and told me that I better open the front door because there was a special package out there for me. I was so excited. I put on my bathrobe and went to the door. I saw a box with holes in the sides of it. My heart began to beat fast. I wondered, could there be an animal inside? Could it finally be the dog I'd always wanted?

I promised myself I would be nice to my parents forever if there was a dog inside. Especially if it was a poodle.

I was afraid to look. Maybe it would be a rabbit. I wouldn't want to hurt their feelings, but I didn't want a rabbit. They need to live in a cage in the basement or outside and they have funny beady red eyes. My mom said, "Don't you want to see what's inside?"

And then I heard a whimper like puppies make. I was so happy. I opened the box and there was a shivering, whimpering, black poodle puppy! I couldn't believe it. My mom had kept her promise!

I started to cry. I took the puppy out of the box and held her in my arms. She was shivering but started to lick my face right away and even though it tickled so badly, I instantly loved her. She snuggled against me and stopped shivering. I knew at that moment that I was going to be happy forever. My parents were smiling and looking at me and holding hands. I felt so good inside. Now I have a puppy to love. My parents are happy. It was just a perfect belated birthday gift and that's the truth.

Dear Diary,

I named my poodle Fifi—the same as my toy poodle. She's so cute. She licks me all the time and has these beautiful black eyes that shine. Sometimes I just lie on my bed with the real Fifi on my stomach and my toy Fifi by my head and I just think how happy I am. When I'm at school or sleeping, we leave Fifi barricaded in the kitchen and laundry room—at least until she's fully trained. When we're home she already goes to the back door when she needs to go outside. She's so smart. My mom said she's all my responsibility. I don't mind. Responsibility is part of being older—and this is one thing I'm happy to be responsible for!

I sent tons of pictures of Fifi to Angela and all the girls. The best pictures were of me holding her in my arms, like a baby. She looks up at me with such love in her dark eyes. I finally have someone to love who isn't going to tell me what to do or yell at me or annoy me. I am so happy right now. This makes the move a little bit easier.

Dear Diary,

I hate Sally. I thought she was just ignoring me. Well, today it got worse. She laughed as I walked by and said something about how I look like a toad. It didn't make any sense what she said, except that my sweater was green and maybe toads are green, too. But after she said that I felt miserable. All day I felt more and more ugly, hearing her chuckle and replaying her words in my head.

When I got home I lay down on my bed and couldn't move. I felt like everything good about me was sucked away. Finally, I had to get up for supper. My parents asked what was wrong. I didn't tell them. It felt too bad to even share.

Later, after eating almost nothing but some peas (I love peas, no matter what), I got an idea. I went into the bathroom with my phone and locked the door. I started to take selfies in the mirror. At first it was hard to smile, but after a while I felt a little better. I not only smiled, but I began to pose like I used to when I used to love looking at myself in the mirror. That was when I was a little kid, like nine or ten. Anyway, after I took about twenty pictures I emailed some of them to Angela, and she wrote back right away saying how cute I looked! Then she sent me some of herself, and we began to chat online. Soon I felt okay again. I had found a way to get back at Sally.

I also sent a couple of them to Betty Ann. She said she loved them, too.

Dear Diary,

        My uncle is really sick. When my dad told me he got that look in his eyes, like when he was so sad last year. I asked him if Uncle Dave (he's not really our uncle, but Dad's best friend who we call "Uncle") is going to die and he said he didn't know. But then he turned away. Dad goes to see him about once a week after work and comes home late at night. I feel really bad on those nights. I just feel empty, knowing that Uncle Dave is lying in a bed in a nursing home feeling so sick and that my dad is feeling so sad when he comes home. I guess he has to fake being happy when he's with my uncle so the sadness comes out when he gets home.

        I wish this had never happened. Why would a nice man like my uncle get so sick? He never swears or is nasty or mean. He always sends me money for my birthday and he always brings me lollipops in the shapes of animals when he visits, even though I am too old for them. But it was still a sweet thing to do. And I'll tell you a secret: I loved those lollipops even when I was eleven. That's when he last came to our house. He's been sick for a long time.

Tonight Dad goes to see him again. Maybe I'll be able to fall asleep before I hear the garage door open and then I won't have to feel sad in my bed when I hear Dad come home.

Dear Diary,

Something good has happened. I don't know why, but my parents are fighting a lot less. Maybe it's because they're so much happier here. Or maybe it's because my room is three rooms away from their bedroom and I can't hear through the walls as much as I did in our old house. Whatever it is, it's wonderful. I feel so much better about them. Maybe they finally realized that fighting is stupid. I hope so!

The only bad part is that stupid baby. I don't want another sibling. When I was little I did and look what I got! My brother. And he's no fun most of the time. So what do I have to look forward to with a new baby—especially one that's a girl? Only someone my parents can love more than me. The baby is due next month. I'm thirteen, and the baby will be zero months. Guess who'll get all the love and attention? Not me.

My grandma keeps saying when she calls, "Soon you'll have a new baby sister! Isn't that wonderful?" What am I supposed to say to her on the phone? "No, it's terrible"?

I tell Fifi about how much I hate the thought of the new baby, but she doesn't know what to say back to me. She just licks me. At least she cares. I wish I had someone to talk to about this, like a best friend. A new best friend would understand. A new best friend would know there are feelings I can't tell my parents or my grandmother, ever.

I've told Angela everything I'm telling you, either on the phone or on email, but still, since we don't see each other in person, it doesn't feel like the kind of relief I really need. And Betty Ann just won't do. I like her—kind of—but she is so brainy and so busy with her homework. I think I won't really have a new best friend around here, especially not until I stop being with Betty Ann all the time. The other girls definitely don't like her very much.

Dear Diary,

Angela invited me back to Springport for a weekend sleepover. I'm going in two weeks, right after Thanksgiving. Grandma told me she will take me and pick me up. But I'm scared, which is kind of surprising. I thought I would want to go back and see her and my old friends and old neighborhood, but I'm not sure now. I'm just getting used to living here. And now I have four friends, including, of course, Betty Ann. She's fun and calls me at night, but I know she's not going to ever be a best friend like Angela is.

My other friends, Jackie, Sally, and Joan, I met in gym class. We all started to laugh hysterically in the locker room over something silly. I can't even remember what it was. And now we're good friends. I've already been over to Jackie's house twice and Sally and Joan came, too. We just have so much fun together. When we aren't laughing we're looking at magazines like Seventeen and planning what we're going to wear when we're older and what makeup we'll use. Or we're eating potato chips and popcorn and dancing in the living room.

We are trying new dance styles like they have on <u>Dancing with the Stars</u>, which is Joan's favorite show. Since there are four of us we can dance in pairs. We dance so fast and sometimes we pull each other down on the rug and just laugh and tickle each other. I sweat a lot when we dance, but I don't care. I love the way I feel moving so fast and holding on as one of us turns. This is better than ballet. I think I want to be a ballroom dancer when I grow up.

I don't know what to do about going to see Angela. Maybe I won't go. Sally invited all of us sleep over at her house that weekend. I want to go to Sally's. I don't want them to get together without me. I'm confused about exactly what I want—and who I want to spend my time with—and that's the truth.

Dear Diary,

I can't believe that I've been going to my new school for almost three months already. Most of the time I have to take the school bus in the morning. That means walking two blocks and waiting in line at the curb. The kids on the bus make so much noise—I can't stand it. I usually sit with Caren. She's sort of nice, but not really. I think she is spoiled. She's an only child. Even though she's in seventh grade she has braids down to her waist. I think she looks silly and babyish wearing her hair like that. Maybe she's just sheltered, as my mom would say.

I don't want to really hang around Caren. The problem is that she's the only girl who lives near me. Jackie, Sally, and Joan live in South Ridge. I'm the only kid my age in this neighborhood. I wish my parents had moved to South Ridge instead. Sometimes I worry that Jackie, Sally, and Joan won't like me as much because I don't live closer to them. I hope that isn't true. They are some of my best friends ever.

The boys all sit in the back of the bus and the girls are in the front. I don't know why. The boys fall off their seats into the aisle all the time. I don't know why they fall off, either. I think it's because they clown around all the time. They're disgusting. There is one cute boy, but I'm not ready to talk about him yet.

Actually, all the older boys in my school are disgusting. They have such loud voices and push through the halls, not caring if they push you against the lockers. They swear all the time as they walk down the halls, too. I can't believe it. They are worse than my cousin who can't control his swearing! I hate them. The boys my age are much nicer but they're so short and look so babyish! Ugh!

Dear Diary,

Well, now I'm ready to talk about it.
I'm in love!

I realized how much in love I am
over Thanksgiving weekend. I didn't
get to see the boy I like on the
school bus and even the delicious
turkey my grandma made couldn't
keep me from thinking only about him. I
missed just seeing his smile twice a day on
the bus. His name is Rob, and he's so cute. I
can't believe I found him. He's not in my class,
because he is a year older. He's fourteen. I
don't know why I didn't notice him right away
on the bus, but now I have a hard time not
looking at him.

Here's what he looks like: He has brown hair
and deep blue eyes. He's about six inches taller
than I am—finally, a tall boy! If he invites me
to a dance I won't have to look over his head
across the room when we dance, like I had to
with Paul.

He stands very straight and smiles a lot.
And he doesn't swear like lots of the older

boys. I hate when they swear. He's refined—at least that's what my mom told me he is when I described him to her today. He has a best friend, Brian. Jackie, my new best friend, is in love with Brian so we have a lot to talk about.

He hasn't really noticed me yet but he will. I just know he will.

I've never been so in love before. Even with Paul it wasn't this much. I think about Rob morning, noon, and night.

And guess what? I made my mom drive me by his house so I could see where he lives. He has a nice house. It has a one-car garage. His family has a green car. I see it in the driveway. I think it's a Buick.

Someday he'll take me to the Teen Town Dance and his father will drive us there in that car! I just know it, and that's the truth.

Dear Diary,

I have a secret and it's been eating me up inside, so I have to tell you. I lied to Angela. I told her I had a terrible sore throat and couldn't come for the weekend. She said she was sorry and that she would invite me again. I felt terrible, and then my throat really began to hurt. But I just couldn't go to Springport for a whole weekend—even though I miss being around Angela.

Now that I have best friends here, I don't feel the same way I used to about going back to visit. And I didn't know how to tell Angela that. I could tell when we talked on the phone that she really wanted me to come. And she sent me a new selfie, holding a sign that reads I Miss You! She even told me that she doesn't have a new best friend since I left. She really misses me. She also told me that Paul is in lots of her classes and he asks if she's talked to me. How could I tell her I'm in love with Rob and don't care about Paul anymore? How could I tell her that I have new best friends and want to stay here with them?

I did go to Sally's instead, and we had the best time. Her mother ordered pizza for us and we drank Coke. We watched television and made popcorn and did each other's hair with all of Sally's older sister's hair products we found in the bathroom. I look silly with curly hair.

We kept laughing and falling on the floor and giggling, and we played this fun game that Jackie learned in camp last summer. We all lay down on the floor and we each put our head on someone else's belly. Someone says, "Ha-ha," and then the next person says, "Ha-ha-ha," until everyone is laughing. Then you can't stop laughing because the belly you are on is bouncing all around under your head.

Sally's mom got really angry at all the noise we were making, and we had to turn off the lights and pretend to go to sleep. I hardly slept a wink, though. I was so excited and having so much fun with my new friends.

I was tired the next morning and really did have a sore throat when I went home, but I didn't care. It was worth it to have so much fun.

Dear Diary,

My mom went to the hospital this morning. I got up and I heard her crying and running around the house like a mad woman. I got scared and asked her what was wrong. She told me that she was having contractions and nothing was wrong. But she looked like a lot was wrong. She looked awful! Her hair was wild and her clothes were all wet. She said that her water had broken and then yelled at Dad to hurry up, because she had to get to the hospital. NOW. I don't know what that meant, about her water breaking, but it sounded a bit scary.

Mom practically screamed at me that I had to watch my brother and then she threw on her coat. Dad picked up her suitcase (which has been packed for their trip to the hospital for over a week now) and they left. And there my brother and I were, all alone in the house.

Fifi was running in circles. I guess she was scared, too. I made breakfast for the two of us and fed Fifi. Then I watched my brother until he got on the bus. I had already missed my school bus so I just hung around waiting to hear from my dad. I'd have to make up my school work over the weekend, I guess.

I had nothing to do. Fifi fell asleep and I just wandered around the house wondering if anything would ever be the same again. The next time I would see my mom there would be a baby with her, too.

I have a secret. I don't want a baby sister. I want my mom to be okay. I want her to be just the same, not busy taking care of a baby. I don't want the baby to die or anything awful like that. I just don't want it. I think I've been in denial (a term my grandmother told me once) about the baby coming home. Does that make me a bad person?

Dear Diary,

It's midnight now. I can't sleep so I'm writing to you. Around one o'clock in the afternoon, after I made myself a peanut butter and jelly sandwich and watched two soap operas on TV, my dad finally called and told me to get ready, he was coming home to take me to the hospital.

We had to go right away so I could get back in time to watch my brother. Kids under ten aren't allowed at the hospital during visiting hours for some reason. So he has to wait until mom comes home in five days to see her and the baby. But Dad said he would take some pictures and get them developed. He told me my mom was fine and that I have a beautiful baby sister.

I started to cry. I didn't know if I was happy or sad, and that's the truth.

I ran into my bedroom and got my locket out of my night table drawer and put it on. I felt better as soon as it was on me.

When we got to the hospital I was so scared. I wanted to hate the baby and I wanted to love it at the same time. I asked my dad what the baby's name was. He said, "Gloria." Can you believe that? I already hated one Gloria from when we lived in Springport! Now I was going to meet another one and I couldn't ever get rid of this one. Ugh.

My mom was sleeping when I arrived. My dad said she had worked so hard that she was very tired and needed to rest. What kind of work did she do? I thought they put you to sleep to have a baby. Now I'm really scared. I don't know if I ever want to have a baby. You can't ignore a baby. If you're the mom and it wakes you up, you have to get up even if it means you're exhausted the next day. I hate to be tired.

We went down to the nursery. There were a ton of babies. It looked like everyone had a baby today.

Then there she was. My sister. They brought her up to the window. She was wrapped in a pink blanket and had the same color hair I have. She looked so small and cute! I started to cry again and to laugh at the same time.

Now I have another secret: I think I like Gloria.

I'm all mixed up inside like a cake mixer is in my stomach. I hated her a few hours ago and now I kind of like her. Grandma came to stay with us tonight so we wouldn't be alone so much. But I can't tell her my feelings. She thinks another baby is just wonderful. She loves having more grandchildren. That's all she has to do anyway—visit and take care of grandkids.

It's not that simple for me. I have a lot of other things I have to do.

Dear Diary,

Mom and Gloria came home from the hospital today. Mom had to stay two extra days because of something that happened. I don't know what, but Dad said she is fine now. When they got home, the baby was all wrapped up in blankets and my brother was leaping around the living room like a frog. He was so excited. He kept screaming, "I have a baby sister and her name is Gloria!" He makes me sick.

My grandmother was crying and taking pictures with her new phone when they came in the door. Fifi was barking and Dad put her in the basement. I just pretended I had to go to the bathroom. I felt a little sick inside. I stayed in the bathroom a long time and sat on the toilet, rubbing my locket and trying not to cry. Finally, I knew I had to come out. Grandma and Mom were looking for me. They called out, "Are you okay?"

Of course I said I was all right and that I just had a bit of a tummy ache. When I finally flushed the toilet my mom had already put

Gloria into the bassinet in her room. Mom came up to me and gave me a big hug and kiss and said, "Thanks for being my number one daughter. I love you so much, and I know you'll be such a help to me and the baby."

She looked tired but pretty. I felt good that she said that. I felt really good that she was home.

I need my mom and that's the truth.

Dear Diary,

I am so sick of Christmas carols. My mom loves them and we have been hearing them at home for the last two weeks. She must have every CD ever made that has Christmas carols on it. A whole bunch of cousins and Grandma and Grandpa came over on Christmas Day. It was kind of nice. The house finally felt like it was our home. The gas fireplace in the living room was on all day, and the tree had all of its decorations on it from our old house, plus a bunch of new ones that Dad brought home.

I got a lot of presents this year. Of course, I got the standard gifts, things like pajamas and scarves and two gift certificates. But there was a special present from Santa Claus (my brother still believes so we have to be careful not to ruin it for him). You know what it was? A new computer. The note from Santa said, "I hope the whole family enjoys this computer, especially the young lady living here who I heard is quite a good student. It came to my attention at the North Pole that the family computer was breaking down a lot. This computer was manufactured by elves at my factory in the North Pole and is guaranteed for at least five years." We all laughed about that note, except my brother, who was upset that he wasn't directly mentioned by Santa. Mom had to hug him for a while until he forgot all about the computer and found a few more presents under the tree that were for him.

Dear Diary,

I was so worried that Gloria would cry all night and wake me up, but so far she hasn't. At least I don't hear her. And she's already more than three weeks old!

Jackie told me a secret today. She said that she hated her brother Fred when he was a baby. She was afraid to tell her parents because they seemed to love him so much. But he made her sick every time she looked at him. He made such stupid faces and spit up all the time. He cried a lot and she got a lot less attention after he was born. She was eight years old when he was born. She told me that she cried herself to sleep lots of times and really believed that her parents loved him better than her. She told me that she still gets jealous of him sometimes. Once when he was little she hid his favorite action figure for a week. He was crying all the time and looking all over for it. Finally she felt so guilty that she put it back in his pile of toys. He was so excited when he found it and kept saying, "But I looked there before and it wasn't there!"

She never told anyone what she did.

I was five when my brother was born and I don't remember much about it. But it was good to hear Jackie tell the truth about her little brother. It made me feel like we are really best friends now.

Nothing can ever come between us.

Dear Diary,

On the bus today Rob was wearing a blue sweater with red stripes. He looked so handsome. He wears eyeglasses sometimes—I don't know why. He has very blue eyes. Paul had brown eyes. I like Rob's better. I think he is even taller than when I first saw him. His teeth are very white. Mine aren't. I keep brushing them but my mom told me that some people just don't have pure white teeth.

I wish I had whiter teeth. I wish I didn't have a space between my two front teeth. Some of the kids are wearing braces now. My mom had my teeth checked and the dentist said I don't need braces. "There's nothing wrong with a little space. You have healthy teeth," he said.

But there is something wrong. I want to look perfect. I don't want yellowish teeth and a space between my front teeth. What if Rob notices that my teeth aren't really white? He might never ask me to a dance. I feel miserable.

Dear Diary,

    After supper last night my mom said that we're going to start a new tradition. If anybody is sad or upset all they have to do is call out "Family Hug" and everyone who is home has to run to the person who called it out. Then we all have to stand in a group together and hug each other. So it's like one big giant family hug.

    We all tried it. It was fun. First I got to call out, then my brother, then my mom, and then my dad. Each time we all ran and found each other and stood in a circle and hugged each other. Then the last time we pretended that Gloria had called out and we got her out of her infant seat and included her in the hug.

    It really felt good to do all those hugs.

    This morning I asked my mom where she and Dad came up with that idea. She said that she had read about it in a parenting magazine.

    Sometimes my mom is very smart. I really love the hugs. I hope we do them a lot. They always make you feel better, no matter what. And that's the truth.

Dear Diary,

 Dad went to see Uncle Dave again. He told us that Uncle Dave is very sick and that we might never see him again. Then he started to cry. Mom asked, "Why don't we pray for Uncle Dave to get well." And then she said, "You know, Harold, we really should join a congregation. The children need a place to go where they can learn all about the Bible and God."

 Dad got this angry look on his face and just walked out of the room. He said, "God hasn't been very kind to Dave. Dave has been my best friend since we were six. There isn't a mean bone in his body!"

 Mom just stood there holding the baby and looking upset. I felt terrible. I think Dad was wrong to walk out on us like that. We need him to stay with us when bad things happen. I hate my dad sometimes. Today was one of those times.

 And I also know in my heart that Uncle Dave is going to die soon and there's nothing that anyone can do or say that will make it better. And that is a bad truth.

Dear Diary,

Jackie has a secret and I can't wait until I go over to her house on Friday when she promised to tell me what it is. What could it be? She won't even give me a clue. She just kept saying over the phone that it was a surprise. Sally and Joan can't come this weekend so it's just the two of us. I'm so excited. I love surprises.

I've got a secret, too. I'm so happy that Sally and Joan aren't coming over. I like Jackie the best, and sometimes I get jealous when the others are there. I know we're all supposed to be best friends, but I love being alone with Jackie. We laugh so much and tell secrets all the time. Some of the secrets I'm not even telling you. But I'll give you a clue. A lot of the secrets are about what our husbands will be like and how it will be when we are grown-ups.

When I go over there we mostly eat snacks, watch television, dance in the living room, and look at fashion magazines. Friday we're going to look at the new <u>Seventeen</u> magazine and maybe <u>Vogue</u>. I can't wait to see what I should be wearing this spring. I love to imagine myself really being seventeen and dressed up just like the models in the magazine.

When we get into bed that's the best time. Jackie has a big double bed and we both sleep in it. But before we fall asleep we tell even more secrets. I cannot wait until Friday night!

Dear Diary,

I had a great time at Jackie's house. I learned what her secret is. She got her period a couple of days ago. She told me every detail. She woke up in the morning and felt like she was peeing in bed. But when she looked at the sheet there was blood on it. She got scared and ran to get her mother. Her mother started laughing and said, "No, you just got your period. You're not bleeding to death!"

Then her mother helped her in the bathroom and they changed the sheets together. Jackie said she had to bring a little bag with stuff in it to change at school. I hate that idea. What if someone sees what I have in my backpack? I'd die of embarrassment.

Jackie doesn't have her period anymore. It lasted only two days, which her mother said happens with young girls. I asked Jackie if she felt any different. She said, "No."

When we told secrets in bed that night I didn't tell her one of mine that I'll tell you. It's the one about getting my period. I don't want to get my period and not be a girl anymore.

I don't feel ready to be a woman, which is what my mom says you'll be once you get your period. I want to get older, but I don't want all this extra stuff. Can you understand that? It's confusing, I know. I'm even confused about it.

Dear Diary,

My mom came into my room this morning as I was getting dressed. She said, "I think it's time for you to get a training bra."

I looked at her and said, "I don't want to 'train' anything except Fifi."

She laughed and said, "But all girls have to wear training bras. It's just an expression. Maybe we can go shopping back in Springport. Wouldn't that be fun?"

I mumbled, "Yeah."

She left because the baby was crying. After she left I started to cry also. I really don't want to wear a bra, ever. And that's the truth.

Dear Diary,

When I was little I heard my song in my head all the time, but as I got older it just seemed to leave. I knew it was mine because I never heard it anywhere else except in my head.

Today I remembered it for just a minute. The last time was when I sang it to my mom when we were out walking. That was years ago.

But today I was listening to music from a musical called Kismet. There's a part of the music where it suddenly goes to a high note and sounds very romantic. A man was singing it. All of a sudden I had a strange feeling in my stomach, like an ache. It was a good ache. And it was almost the way my song had gone up to a high note.

I wish I could really remember my song. It feels empty not to have it inside me anymore.

    I wrote a poem. Maybe it can be a song about my song:

    I have a song
    I hear it inside
    Listen to me
    Can you hear it too?
    Oh, don't say, "No."
    Even for me, it comes and goes
    And I'm so afraid
    'Cause no one seems to know
    My song!
    I'm getting older and it seldom comes.
    What is in store for me
    As I get older?

    Dear Diary, do you like it? Maybe someday I will email the song to Angela or tell Jackie about it. But right now it is our secret. Okay?

Dear Diary,

I'm so upset. I lost my locket! I went to put it on this morning and it wasn't in the drawer with my ring and my wristwatch and the bracelet with the heart on it. I don't remember taking it off anywhere else. But it's gone.

I don't know what to do. That locket means so much to me. Aunt Belinda will be so disappointed in me to think I lost it. It's really the most precious thing I have.

I'm miserable. I keep walking around the house looking for it. I've gone through my dresser drawers about ten times. I keep looking through my backpack and my purse. I looked under my bed and even through my sister's and brother's things.

I feel so bad. There will never in the whole world be another locket like mine. And that's the truth.

Please, someone help me find my locket!

Dear Diary,

Phew! I found my locket. It was under my bed. I decided to look on the floor all over my room one more time. I got down on my hands and knees and pretended I was a puppy sniffing around, like Fifi. It was fun. All of a sudden I saw something bright and shiny behind one of the legs to my bed. I couldn't believe it at first. My heart was pounding as I reached for it. It was my locket. I don't know it got there. Maybe I forgot and went to sleep with it on. My mom said I might have taken it off in my sleep and dropped it. Anyway, I feel so happy. I couldn't stand the way I felt. I hope I never lose it again.

Dear Diary,

Today we went back to Springport, my mom and me. My dad watched the baby and my brother went to a neighbor's. I called Angela and we picked her up and took her out to lunch. It was funny to see her again—it's been so long. She gave me a big hug and kiss. I kissed her back and we both started laughing and looking at each other. She's much taller now and her breasts are too large for a training bra. Her hair is short and fluffy and she's wearing a little bit of makeup, too.

We ate lunch at the Towne Diner. It was our favorite restaurant when we lived here. I got a hamburger, french fries, and a coffee-flavored milkshake.

Angela told me all about the other kids at school. Gloria's parents got divorced and she stays at her aunt's house a lot. She stopped taking dance class. So I guess she won't be a ballerina when she grows up after all.

Angela will be moving to upstate New York, finally, in three months. So then we both will be gone from Springport—and I'll be even farther away from her.

Angela also told me that Paul suddenly started to grow. She said she thinks he's as tall as me now. Wow. That's a shock!

I wanted to see him today but I also didn't want to see him. After all, I love Rob now. I don't want to love two boys at the same time. That would be too confusing. Plus, Paul lives too far away.

After lunch my mom insisted that we go to Reid's department store, and guess what? She bought me two training bras. Angela came into the changing room with me and told me that I really do need them. I guess everybody but me believes in training your chest.

I made my mom drive by Rob's house on our way home. He was in the driveway washing his dad's car. I thought I would die. He saw me and waved.

Now, how can I keep driving by his house? He lives on a side street and really there's no reason for my mom to be driving me down that street. This is awful. I just wanted to be near him, not to have him see me! I'm miserable and that's the truth.

Dear Diary,

My mom told me that she's going to take me out for supper once every other week. She said she'll also take my brother out, but at a different time. Thank goodness. I would <u>hate</u> to go at the same time as him. He's such a jerk, whining and complaining and wanting to stay up late just because I do. After all, I'm five years older than he is! He just has to wait until he's old enough.

So tomorrow night Mom and I are going to go out to Jack Marano's Restaurant. It's an Italian restaurant near our house. I'm so excited. Mom said I can order whatever I want. I know exactly what I want—eggplant parmigiana. It will be a nice new tradition, and I'm excited to have the time with my mom all by myself. And that's the truth!

Dear Diary,

Mom and I went out tonight to Jack Marano's. It was wonderful. We sat in a wooden booth all by ourselves. There was this really handsome older waiter who waited on us. He kind of treated us like a queen and princess. I think he must have been at least forty, maybe even forty-five years old. But he was pretty good looking even if he was old.

I was so busy talking to my mom about Rob that I almost forgot to order. The waiter actually had to stand there awhile and finally said, "Excuse me, miss, would you like to order?"

I felt embarrassed because he heard everything I was saying about Rob. But what does it matter? We don't know him and he doesn't know us.

I had to tell my mom exactly what Rob had been wearing and what he said on the bus yesterday. I overheard him tell his friend Brian (that's the guy that Jackie thinks is so cute) that he will be mowing lawns all over the neighborhood in the spring. I guess he will be making a lot of money! I begged my mom to ask Dad if we can hire him to mow our lawn, but she said that for now Dad wants to do it himself. She also said I could help mow it if I want to. Is she crazy? Why would I want to if Rob could mow the lawn for us? Then I would see him even more. I could stand in the window where he couldn't see me and watch him push the lawn mower.

I told my mom that I love him so much, more than I ever loved Paul. She just smiled and let the waiter serve her meatballs and spaghetti. Why does she always just smile when I tell her things like this?

The eggplant parmigiana was so delicious. The melted cheese was kind of crusty and the layers of eggplant were so tasty. I ate every bite. It came in a casserole dish that they cooked it in. I can't wait to go out again with my mom. And I'm going to keep harassing them about asking Rob to mow our yard. I just have to!

Dear Diary,

    Why do I hate to look at myself in the mirror sometimes? I used to love to look at myself. I even played dress-up in front of it. Now I feel so rotten when I look at myself. I see everything. I see too many freckles on my face. I see my teeth looking back at me, not pearly white but slightly yellow with a space between the front teeth that looks larger every time I examine it. I don't feel like taking any selfies anymore. Angela wants me to send her some of me with the baby, but I don't want to. I just don't like the way I look right now. I see big ears even though my mom said I don't have big ears. And I see fat on my body. Baby fat is not cute at thirteen. My mom keeps saying that I'll be thinner once I get my period. She also reminds me that it must be coming very soon since I'm cranky a lot. I get so angry when she says that.

    Here are some more secrets: I'm miserable. Why don't I just feel good about myself like I used to when I was younger? Why can't I just read a Nancy Drew book or get on my bicycle

and feel so much better? Nothing is the same.
Will it ever get better again? Will I ever feel like
my old self?

Dear Diary,

The worst thing in the whole world happened. Uncle Dave died yesterday. I can't believe it. He seemed old to me, but I guess grown-ups think he was young. He was forty-six, the same age as my dad. Forty-six is old, but not old enough to die!

Dad's in a horrible mood. His whole face looks awful, like he has a fever. And he's walking around all slumped over. I feel so bad for him. I feel bad for the rest of us also, because it isn't fun to have a sad dad around. And I'm scared. This is the first funeral I've ever been to. Dad said I'm old enough to go. Mom said I should wear my black skirt and my dark gray sweater. I hate both of those things, and I planned to give the sweater away. But she said you're supposed to look somber at a funeral, and I guess that's the only somber things I have to wear—thankfully.

Tomorrow we'll go to the funeral home at 2:00 pm. I get to miss school. This is one time I wish I could go to school instead.

Afterwards we have to go to the graveyard

and watch them bury the casket. This is awful. As soon as I finish writing I'm going to go to bed. I hope I don't have nightmares about Uncle Dave and the funeral and all that. I wish Angela was here. She'd know how to make me feel better. Maybe I should email Jackie and tell her before I go to bed.

Dear Diary,

It's over. The worst day of my life so far. We went to Uncle Dave's funeral and we went to the graveyard and we went to a restaurant with all the relatives afterward.

The only good part about the funeral was the casket was closed. Dad said that the family chose to have it closed since Uncle Dave had been so sick. I think that was a wise choice. Who wants to see a dead person anyway? Of course his whole family was there and that was so sad to see. He wasn't married, but both his parents are still alive and they looked so miserable. My mom told me that the worst thing in the world for a parent is to lose a child! I guess even a child that old!

The funeral was awful. Everyone was crying. Everyone looked bad. At least they didn't have any children so there were no little kids to cry.

I felt empty inside. It was a worse feeling than the first day we moved when I felt so alone.

The graveyard was also awful. The wind was blowing and it was cold. I hugged my mom and held my dad's hand. In a way it was nice, because we were so close and Gloria and my brother were home with a babysitter. Just the three of us went through this.

I didn't eat anything at the restaurant except coffee-flavored ice cream. I had no appetite. I just played with my locket while the grown-ups talked.

I hope I don't have to go to any more funerals for a long time. I wish people didn't die. Why can't we all live forever?

Dear Diary,

Since my Uncle Dave died I've been having strange dreams. I can't really remember them but I wake up feeling bad. Except last night when I woke up suddenly and instead of feeling bad I felt excited. I couldn't believe it. I had a poem in my head and it wouldn't go away.

So I decided I better get up and write it down. I got a pencil and a notebook out of my backpack and wrote. Here is the poem:

The wind was blowing through the trees
The ships were tossing on the seas
And as I lay awake in bed
I had thoughts of things I dread

But then sweetness surrounded me
And angels were singing above my head
I was suddenly at peace and fell into
A blissful sleep I pray I can keep!

I think there were more lines but I forgot them. I read the poem to my parents in the morning. They were surprised. My dad looked almost like he was going to cry. Dad said the poem made him feel a little better even though he still can't wrap his mind around his best friend being so sick and dying. He and Mom both said I should save the poem. I felt happy that somehow I helped Dad feel better. I know I was comforted during the night and maybe that and Dad feeling better is all that matters for now. I've read that angels can come to you and help you feel better. That's what I feel happened to me. Those lyrics came from somewhere, not just me. Anyway, I hope the bad dreams go away soon.

Dear Diary,

I've decided that my behind is definitely too big. I read in <u>Seventeen</u> that you should sit on the floor with your legs in front of you and bounce on your behind as you make yourself walk across the room. I'm starting to do that every night. It feels funny but I don't care. I want my behind to be much smaller. I'm trying to make myself do this for ten minutes each night.

But sometimes I forget to bounce across the room. How will I ever be in shape for the summer? It's already March and I still look gigantic from behind. My mom told me that as soon as I get my period I'll probably drop five pounds of water weight. I hope she's right. I can never be seen in a bathing suit the way I look now, especially not in front of Rob!

Dear Diary,

Today is my birthday! Mom made me my usual birthday dinner of delicious steak and we had a yummy chocolate birthday cake, all decorated. Grandma and Grandpa came over and everyone sang "Happy Birthday." I'll be taking Jackie and the other girls to the movies this Saturday as part of my present. We will be seeing Jersey Boys. Mom and Grandma love the music from Jersey Boys. I think that's because they are old.

Of course there was another gift for me from Aunt Belinda. I hope this won't hurt your feelings, Dear Diary, but it is a gorgeous new diary. I'm sorry to have to tell you this, but you will be finished one of these days. You only have so many pages inside of you. And then, of course, I will need a new diary. Well, Aunt Belinda was thinking ahead, and now I have it. But don't be too sad. I will never forget you! And I will take you out and read your pages

14

every now and then. Meanwhile, you are still my confidante.

Here is my latest secret: I'm saving all of my birthday money (and it is over $150.00) to buy myself a tablet. I can't wait. Then I can surf the web, be on Facebook any time I want to, even in bed, and play games whenever I want. There is one small problem, though. My parents say too much technology is dangerous. They want everything to be like the old days. And Grandma . . . . . it is even worse with her. She keeps telling me how her family only had one phone when she was a kid. And no TV until she was twelve. But that was a long time ago. This is now and I think having a tablet would be so cool.

Dear Diary,

Did I tell you I made the Honor Roll for the third quarter? Mom and Dad were so proud of me. Grandma, too. I was pretty happy myself. It turns out that being a good friend of Betty Ann's has been good for me in terms of my schoolwork. She is so smart and we study together a couple times a week. The other kids aren't as interested in good grades as she is. But I am. I want to go to a good college someday.

She has taught me lots of study habits that I didn't know, like how to memorize vocab words. Here's how you do it: Fold a paper and put the words in the left hand column and the definition in the right hand column. Then look at the word and make yourself say aloud the definition with the paper folded and then do it the other way around. It really works! Maybe for the end of the year I will even make the High Honor Roll!

Dear Diary,

My dad came home tonight and said he had a family announcement to make. We all had to gather in the dining room and sit around the table and listen. My brother looked scared. My mom was holding Gloria on her lap. I put Fifi on my lap.

My dad said, "I've made a family decision. Now that Uncle Dave died I realize that we do need to go to church. It's important to have some sort of faith. I'm not that sure what I believe, but your mother wants you to believe in something. So I've decided that we're going to become Universal Harmony Witnesses."

Everyone looked amazed. I don't know what a Universal Harmony Witness is. I know Catholics and Protestants and I even know a few Jewish kids. But I don't know any Universal Harmony Witnesses.

We were all quiet. My brother just fidgeted and asked if we would have to move. I guess he didn't understand all the grown-up talk.

Mom said, "Well, dear, why would we become that?"

Dad said it was because we have so many backgrounds in our family. We have Catholics and Protestants and our relatives also came from all different places in the world. So the smartest thing to do to be fair to all of our ancestors is to be something else, like Universal Harmony Witnesses.

It still didn't make much sense.

My brother still wanted to know if we had to move again. I said, "Be quiet. It has nothing to do with moving."

Dad said the Universal Harmony Witnesses are very fair and don't put a lot of demands on you, and that lots of people who aren't sure what they are go to services there.

Well, that's about all I got out of the conversation. I just know that we're going next Sunday.

Actually, I'm happy. I like to learn new things and maybe I'll get some answers for the things that are confusing right now for me.

Dear Diary,

We went to the Universal Harmony Witness church today. It was kind of strange. It really wasn't in a church building. It was some sort of Women's Club that they use. They don't have their own building yet. We sat in an auditorium on folding chairs and heard a sermon. I didn't understand some of it and I fell asleep for a while, but I liked the minister. He has a nice smile and he welcomed us. He actually hugged each of us and said he was so happy we came. My brother went to some kids' class during the service but I got to stay with Mom and Dad. Gloria was dropped off at the next-door neighbor's house. They're Chinese and don't go to church on Sundays so they're home. The dad is some sort of really brilliant scientist. They have one kid, a boy, eight years old. He's one of my brother's best friends.

One thing the minister said is that Universal Harmony Witnesses believe in God. I sure was glad to hear that. I thought he said something about not believing in miracles. I was confused about that. I asked my mom and she said that probably he meant that everything is a miracle.

My dad seemed to enjoy the sermon. I'm glad because he's been so sad since Uncle Dave died. It's the first time I saw him smile in a while.

After the service we went downstairs to the basement and had cookies and drinks. A lady told me that when I come again I can go to a class for older kids. Someone else told us that they have a lot of fun things, like potluck suppers. That sounds kind of cool. I didn't see any kids my age but the lady said there are at least five.

There are only about fifty people who come to this church. Angela went to a Catholic church that must have had thousands of people. And Jackie goes to a Methodist church that's almost as big as my school.

Anyway, I'll give this a shot. At least it's nice to get out of the house and meet new people every week.

Dear Diary,

I have a secret. I've been thinking. I'm not sure I want to be a Universal Harmony Witness. I'm not going to tell anyone, though. I think you should feel something special in a church or wherever you want to worship, but I don't feel anything there.

Maybe it's because we're just sitting in a big meeting hall without any decorations. But Anne Frank could feel special feelings even when all she could hear was a bird singing outside. I want to feel special feelings, too, like she did. In a movie I saw people in church kneeling and praying. I think it was a big Catholic church. They all looked like they were feeling close to God. I want to feel that way too when I go to church. I'm confused and there's no one to ask about this. Maybe I'll act sick next Sunday so I won't have to go.

Dear Diary,

    Rob talks to me every now and then on the bus. A couple of times we sat across from each other. I'm actually beginning to think he might have a crush on me! Jackie said that lots of times when you really love someone they get the vibes you are sending out and love you back. I think she might have made that up. But still, I like the way he talks to me. We've chatted a little about school and stuff. And guess what he wants to do when he grows up? He wants to own an Italian restaurant! I think it's really interesting. I can already see myself helping him run it, while our children sit at a table in the back of the restaurant doing their homework until we leave to go home.

Dear Diary,

I wish I could hear my song again. I still haven't found it. I wish someone really understood me. I wish my uncle hadn't died. I wish I could get all my questions answered. I wish Rob really loved me. I wish my teeth were whiter. I wish I could go to overnight camp. I wish I could take piano lessons. I wish I would get my period next fall so I don't have to worry about it during the summer. I wish my behind didn't have puckers on it. I wish my thighs were thinner. I wish I didn't eat so many cookies. I wish Jackie and Sally and Joan will stay my best friends forever. I wish that Jackie would like me better than our other friends. I wish I wouldn't be growing up so fast. I wish school would be over.

Dear Diary,

The other day Mom and I were home alone. Gloria was over Grandma's for the day, to give Mom a break. My brother was at school, and I was home with a cold. But despite the cold, actually the day turned out to be perfect.

For the first time in months Mom and I had a chance to talk. I told her how sometimes I feel so confused and concerned about things. After she gave me a big, long hug, which already really helped, she said that was so normal for my age. Growing up is tough. There are so many changes and lots of things that we have to get used to. Like getting your period, having more responsibilities, even starting a part-time job or doing other chores. She also told me about some of her best friends at my age and what they did together. They laughed and danced and stayed up late and flirted with boys. She was in love at fourteen. I was so shocked. Why hadn't she ever told me before? His name was Steve, and his father owned the local gas station. She started to tell me about kissing him under the back porch, but the phone rang!

I was so mad. She promised to tell me more. I want to know what happened!

We talked a lot about what can be helpful to a kid growing up. She told me that no matter how busy she looks or acts, I should always tell her when I need to talk or be with her. I told her I need her to still tuck me into bed sometimes, just so we can talk and cuddle. She promised she'd do that more.

I also told her how I love to look at cute videos on YouTube that have dogs playing the piano and singing and stuff like that. When I see those videos I feel happy inside.

She said she wants me to share cute stuff like that with her. I promised I would.

It was such a good day! I was almost sorry my cold got better and I had to go back to school. It was a secret day for just the two of us!

Dear Diary,

Next week is the school beach party. I'm so excited. I can't wait. The whole middle school goes. I'll get to see Rob. And he'll get to see me. I have this beautiful black and white two-piece swimsuit that I can't wait to wear. And I've been really good. I've been bouncing on my behind across the living room floor for the last three weeks. My behind hurts a lot but I think it's a little less fat.

The week after the beach party we start summer vacation. The year went by so fast! I'll be in ninth grade when we go back to school in the fall. Springport seems so far away. But my mom told me we're going back one Saturday soon. She wants to shop at Gleaning's. She says it's better than anything around here. She's going to buy me a lot of new summer clothes, too. I'm excited. Angela already moved away so I guess we'll just shop and eat lunch downtown. They have a really nice café with delicious coffee-flavored ice cream. I'll send Angela some selfies of me in Springport. She's lonely and sad, just like I was when we first moved. I'm trying to cheer her up as much as I can.

Jackie is going to overnight camp, and Sally is going to her grandmother's for a month this summer. Joan is helping her parents in their hardware store. Betty Ann is going to a special camp on a college campus for gifted kids. And guess what is happening to me? I have to babysit Gloria and take piano lessons. Right now I hate Gloria. She cries at least once a night and is crawling all around the house. I almost stepped on her the other day. Stupid baby.

I'm hoping that something else good happens this summer for me!

Last night Mom and I went for our dinner out at Jack Marano's. I got my usual eggplant parmigiana. That super polite older waiter waited on us again. It's funny how he always waits on us. I guess that's because we usually sit in the same booth.

Anyway, I told my mom all about how Rob looked today and how I passed him in the hallway and how he said "hello" to me. And how Jackie and I were dying with laughter because we pretended we had forgotten something and turned around just to follow him down the hallway to his next class. She smiled and nodded, but after the waiter took our order she told me the same stuff she used to say when I was in love with Paul. She reminded me that there will be lots of boys before I get married. I don't want to hear that stuff. I just want her to listen 100 percent when I need her to. She is a little better, ever since we had that day together when I had the bad cold.

The waiter always waits patiently until I finish talking about Rob. He sort of stares into space, but I have a feeling he's listening. But what does that matter? He doesn't know who I am or who Rob is. When I stop talking, he says, "May I take your order, Miss?"

He treats me like a princess. I like that.

Dear Diary,

Today was the school end-of-the-year picnic at the beach. You know how much I was looking forward to today! For weeks it's been on my mind. Jackie and I planned everything we were going to do, what we'd wear, how we would do our hair and our makeup. My mom said I was old enough now to wear a little lipstick and a little blush. I was so excited about my new bathing suit and about wearing the lipstick.

And then it was all spoiled. I woke up this morning and I had it! Can you believe of all the days in the year, I get my period for the first time today?! I went into the bathroom when I woke up and I knew it had begun. I called my mom and started to cry. She ran into the bathroom and I showed her. She got all excited and hugged me and said I was now a woman. I didn't feel like a woman. I just felt disappointed and a little achy.

I got out my stuff from my little bag that they gave out in health class. Then I went into the kitchen for breakfast. I knew the day was ruined. How was I going to go swimming wearing you-know-what? I would die of shame. I was so miserable. I was crying and crying. My mom told me to take two Tylenol and still go but just not to go swimming. She said to wear shorts instead. She must be crazy. Doesn't she know that then everyone in school would know that I have my period? Who would go to a beach party and not go into the water? No one, unless their leg was in a cast from having broken it.

I called Jackie this morning and told her I couldn't go. I was crying so much that she couldn't understand me and I had to repeat myself about four times. She understood why I couldn't go. My mom didn't. But Jackie did. She told me that she would miss me and take pictures. She was bringing her new iPhone. I'm so jealous.

I just hung around the house all day. It was a beautiful sunny day, but I stayed inside. My mom asked me to watch Gloria while she went to the store. I did, but I hated being home. And I hate growing up. My stupid period is ruining what could have been the best day of my life. And Rob didn't even get to see me in my two-piece suit!

I guess Gloria isn't so bad. I was crying on the couch while she was sitting next to me. She seemed to understand and leaned against me as if to comfort me.

By the time Jackie called me in the late afternoon I felt better.

She told me that they all had fun and missed me. She told everyone I had a bad cold. She said that Rob and Brian weren't in the same group so I didn't miss anything interesting. She only saw them at a distance. I made her tell me what kind of bathing suit Rob had on. It was navy blue. I bet he looked so wonderful. I wish I could have seen his body. I bet he has nice muscles.

Jackie promised me that we'll go to the beach together when school is out and we'll find out where the kids who are a year older hang out. She reminded me that she's only going to overnight camp for one month. So I won't be that lonely.

I'm excited. Now I have something to look forward to.

Dear Diary,

I didn't make the High Honor Roll, even though I really tried. But something nice happened. My dad and I were coming back from the supermarket, and suddenly my dad cleared his throat. That usually means he has something important to say. And then he said, "I'm very proud of you even though I know you were disappointed that you didn't make the High Honor Roll. I know this past year was hard for you. I never had to move as a kid, but I could see it was hard to leave all your friends behind. And I know you didn't expect to have a baby sister, either. You've been great!"

Then he reached out and squeezed my hand. I squeezed his hand back. I felt really good inside, all filled up with love.

Dear Diary,

An amazing thing happened to me last night. I had this wonderful dream where I was watching an orchestra play and I could hear the whole thing as if it were real. How could I hear a symphony in my mind? I don't even know music like that. But I knew it was a dream and I even made myself listen to the violins and the horns and the drums and I could hear each play their parts alone and then all together.

It was almost as good as remembering my song. Maybe, if I can remember this one, I'll get a new song all my own!

Dear Diary,

I have a secret. I wrote another song about my song. Since my song may never come back again I decided to at least remember it in a song. Here it is:

My song!

I'm getting older and my song hardly comes anymore.

What is in store for me?

How can I leave behind so much of me?

I've got to believe my song will come back.

I've got to believe that I'll be heard.

I've got to believe that

The song I'll be singing

Is my song, loud and clear!

Now I just have to figure out a tune to go with my song. Maybe I'll dream the tune up tonight. If I can dream a whole orchestra playing I should be able to dream a tune that I can use for my words.

Dear Diary,

As far as my new song goes, nothing happened. I didn't hear any music in my sleep last night. Oh, well. Maybe tonight.

But today a lot happened. My mom took me to Springport like she promised and I got some really cute and fashionable clothes in Gleaning's. I got four pairs of shorts, six t-shirts, two bathing suits, and one sundress. I also got a sun hat, sunglasses, and sandals. I'm so excited. I can't wait to go to the beach with Jackie now! We are supposed to go the end of next week. She doesn't leave for camp until Sunday.

The only bad part of shopping was looking at my behind in the three-way mirror. I bounced across the floor almost every night for the last couple of nights but I think it looks bigger than ever. Why do I have to have such a big one? Maybe swimming will help. My mom told me I eat too many Oreo cookies and they go right to my backside! That sounds crazy but I think she may be right. But I love them so much and I'm always so hungry.

Anyway, after we shopped we went to eat in the café and guess who came in with his mother to eat? I couldn't believe it. I wanted to die on the spot. It was Paul! I hadn't seen him since we moved away. Angela was right—he's only about one inch shorter than I am now. And he's still so handsome. I felt some of those old feelings like I wanted to kiss him a lot. But then I thought of Rob and my feelings sort of disappeared, but then suddenly they would come back.

Paul was very nice to me. He asked me how I liked Clarksville. The café was crowded and Paul and his mom sat at a different counter so we didn't say much to each other. I didn't really enjoy my hamburger. I kept thinking about how much I love Rob but how funny I still felt seeing Paul. I think Paul looked at me a few times. I'm not sure, maybe he was just looking out the window behind me. But I felt myself blushing.

After we finished lunch, we stood up and I waved to Paul as we left. He waved back and said, "See ya." That was it. The final end to so many romantic feelings. I felt let down. All the way home I thought about Paul until we were about two miles from home. Then it was as if he just disappeared into the atmosphere, and I

began to think about Rob.
   I thought of another poem:

   Love, it comes and goes
   But the fire still burns
   Deep inside me, it never cools.
   How hot will the winds blow
   Before I have peace of mind?

   I think maybe I'll be a poet when I grow up.
Poems just seem to keep coming out of me from
somewhere. I don't know where. It's weird.

Dear Diary,

I have another secret. I took out all my dolls and locked my bedroom door. Then I lined them up on my dresser and just looked at them and talked to them. I told them how much I miss them and I felt tears in my eyes. I hugged each one of them and put a new outfit on each. I squeezed Cuddles so she could coo a lot and I hugged Cookie. I let both of them open and close their eyes a lot. I even hugged my Vogue dolls: Veronica, Martha, Tony, and Tina, the ones that I made so many outfits for. Even though they are small and stiff and when I played with them I never hugged them before. I hugged them now.

Then I sat down on my bed and cried. I'm not exactly sure why. When I was done I put them all back in the large box in the closet that they stay in. I hope Gloria never finds them. I'll be furious if she hurts them. I want to give them to my own little girl someday. Not Gloria! If she destroys them I will hate her forever.

Dear Diary,

    Jackie called me this morning and asked me what I did yesterday. We both started to laugh hysterically at one point. That's the best part of talking to Jackie. The laughing feels so good. And we never know why we're laughing. I never met anyone else who I can laugh so hard with.

    But when she asked me again what I did yesterday, I lied. I told her that we all went to see my cousins. I don't know why I lied but I just felt I couldn't talk about my dolls and how I played with them yesterday. And even worse, I didn't want to tell her that I was crying. It really is too big a secret, even for Jackie.

    She didn't know I was lying. I could tell. Then I felt even more terrible about it.

Dear Diary,

Last night I shaved my legs for the first time because tomorrow Jackie and I are finally going to the beach. I was going to shave that day I got my "you-know-what." But since I couldn't go to the school beach party, I didn't do it then. My mom gave me a disposable pink razor. She said I can just throw the razor away when I'm done. Does she think I'm not going to really shave? Or only do it once? I'd be an outcast in the whole school if I showed up next year with hairy legs! Eww!

Shaving felt weird. For a minute I missed all my hairs. It was strange not having my light brown fuzz that I've always had. But it's so grown-up to shave. I shaved under my armpits, too. My deodorant

gross hairy leg

stung a little when I put it on after shaving. But I didn't care. It makes me feel older. I can't wait to go to the beach with my new swimsuit. And maybe I'll even see Rob there. I've missed him.

Dear Diary,

Jackie and I went to the beach today. Her mother dropped us off and my dad picked us up. It was wonderful. We lay in the sun for a couple of hours. My mom said to make sure I put on sunscreen and cover myself up. But I didn't listen. I put on oil instead. Jackie said it gives you a better tan.

Well, we got burned! Not too badly because it was cloudy part of the day. But still when I got home I had to put lots of aloe vera on my skin. My dad was angry when he picked us up and saw we were red. He said that was a dangerous thing to do to your skin, that we could have gotten sun poisoning. I didn't care. I felt so grown-up. There we were lying on big beach towels in our bathing suits with all the other older kids. It was wonderful. Rob wasn't there, though. I think he has a summer job but I don't know what it is.

A whole bunch of us went into the water at the same time. We had a giant beach ball and we were throwing it to each other, splashing and laughing, and some of the guys were trying to push us under the water. It was such fun. One of the boys accidentally rubbed his hand over my chest as he lunged for the beach ball. I felt an exciting shock hit my body. I wonder if it really was an accident, but I don't think I really mind if it wasn't.

We played in the water for a long time. Then Jackie and I collapsed on our towels and rested. After that we went for lunch at the hotdog stand. I had a hotdog and french fries, of course.

Jackie promised we'll come back again as soon as she's back from camp. Maybe I'll go with Sally and Joan while she's away, if they're around. I'll miss Jackie. She's the best person to tell secrets to. You are the only one that might know more than her. That's because I can't tell her the stupid stuff like crying over baby dolls and about the Vogue dolls that I used to make clothes for. That's just something I'm not willing to tell her yet. It's kind of embarrassing.

Dear Diary,

Jackie is away at camp. I miss her so much. She promised to write to me once a week, but so far no letter. I guess she's very busy. I'm not. I babysit Gloria and I read novels. I don't read Nancy Drew anymore, though. She seems silly to me now. The books don't deal with the things I'm thinking about. My mom leaves me at the library and I wander around the stacks while she's grocery shopping with Gloria. My brother goes to our town's stupid camp, but at least my parents didn't make me go this summer. The only kind of camp I'd want to go to anyway would be overnight camp with Jackie.

I learned the word "blessing" at the Universal Harmony Witness Church. I like the word. The minister said everything is a blessing in one way or another. I don't understand that, not really. Lots of things are terrible and not blessings. Killing innocent people is not a blessing. But not going to a town camp to swim in a Y pool with tons of kids splashing is a blessing.

Dear Diary,

I love the library. I'm reading novels written for young adults and adults now. The section I often go to is called "Romance Fiction." There must be hundreds of books there. And things happen to all the women. It isn't just the same old stuff like with Nancy Drew—she just solves a new mystery but everything else stays the same. Same boyfriend. Same maid cooking delicious food. Same two girlfriends tagging along.

Now in the romance novels, exciting things happen to the women all the time. Sometimes they fall in love with someone in town, like their dentist or the owner of the department store. Sometimes someone else is already with that person. And then sometimes there's a divorce or more often someone dies and the star of the book is free to be with her true love. I love reading these books even though I don't always understand some of the things they talk about.

The stories make my life feel exciting. Today I'm reading a novel about a young woman who lives near a volcano on a Pacific Island. Her parents were missionaries and she is the only schoolteacher on the island. She falls in love with the new doctor who comes to the island, but he doesn't know she likes him. After the volcano erupts she has to help save people and she becomes like a nurse. She and the doctor work side by side and of course they fall in love. They marry and stay on the island to help rebuild it and teach and care for everyone. It is the most thrilling story with lots of romance and kissing and caressing. I hide the romance books under my mattress, though, so no one sees them at home. My mom thinks I'm borrowing more mysteries. I always put a Nancy Drew book or another mystery book for kids on top of my books when my mom picks me up from the library, so she doesn't know what I'm actually reading. I feel a little guilty hiding this from her but I don't think she'd understand or like what I'm wanting to read right now. So it's my secret (and only you know anything about it).

Dear Diary,

Jackie's letter finally came from camp. She'll be home in two weeks. In the letter she said that she has an amazing secret and I'm the only one she's telling it to. I'm writing to you part of what she said: "I did two things at camp that my mother would be furious about. I made out with Larry. He is a year older than us. He touched my sweater right on my chest. I moved his hand away fast. Then I smoked a cigarette with him. I loved every minute of it. I feel guilty but so alive. And he promises to write to me. I don't like Brian anymore. You can still like Rob if you want to. But Larry is wonderful. I have a picture to show you when I come home. Don't dare tell anyone. Swear to me you won't. I miss you. Love, Jackie."

I am shocked but so excited. I can't wait to hear all the details. I wonder if she'll do even more stuff with Larry or the other kids before she comes home. She is fourteen and a half. I'm one half year younger than she is.

I bet she does more. I feel it in my bones. I never really even kissed a boy. Is that bad? Should I have done that by now? Is something wrong with me?

Dear Diary,

My parents asked me if I want to go to my Aunt Belinda's house for a week, since I have nothing else to do this summer. I'm shocked. She lives in Minnesota, which is a long way away. My dad said, "You're fourteen. No reason why you can't fly there by yourself. We will make sure that the flight attendants take good care of you."

My mom added, "You should have fun. Aunt Belinda has a great big house and lots of farm animals, and there are some girls your age down the street. It would be better than moping around here."

So guess what? I'm going next week. I'm scared. I've never been on a big plane before. That little plane I flew in when we went to Florida was only for two people. I'm excited and nervous. Maybe there will be someone sitting next to me whose hand I can hold if I need to. Like a nice grandmother. Now I really do have an adventure to write about!

Thursday night I'm going back to Jack Marono's restaurant with Judy and Sally.

It's Joan's birthday and we're celebrating by Joan's mom taking us to dinner. Then when Jackie comes back and I come back from my aunt's we'll have a sleepover at Joan's, with cake and ice cream. I can't wait! And I can't wait to tell Jackie all about Minnesota once I'm back!

Dear Diary,

We went to Jack Marono's. The girls couldn't believe it when I told them that I'm going on a plane to Minnesota by myself!

"Wow. You're so lucky. Your parents treat you like a grown-up," Judy said.

Sally said, "So far I've only been to Brooklyn and Washington, D.C., and that was just because we were invited to family weddings and had to drive my grandmother. She's too old to get there by herself."

I told them I was really excited and that maybe next summer they could come with me (though I'd really just want Jackie to come instead).

When we ordered I got eggplant parmigiana. And guess what? That same older waiter came over to wait on us. He seemed to recognize me and gave me a smile and almost a little wink. I felt a little embarrassed because just as he came over, guess who I was talking about? Rob. This time I was telling the girls how I saw him in the car with his mother a few days ago. He passed right by me as I was walking in front of the library. He was wearing a red striped shirt. He looked so cute. He got a short haircut for the summer. He looked so hot. The waiter was just as polite as ever, waiting for me to finish what I was saying before he took the order. I just had the funniest feeling that he was getting a kick out of what I was saying, but I don't know why. Maybe he just likes kids.

I had so much fun at dinner. Now I have to pack. I can't wait to go and see Aunt Belinda! And maybe I'll meet some fun girls there, too!

Dear Diary,

    I've been at my Aunt Belinda's for a couple of days. The plane trip was easy. Even when the plane bumped up and down I didn't need to hold any one's hand or throw up. I just read my book and stared out the window at all the clouds and, when there was a break in them, the farmland below.

    Of course I brought you with me. How could I travel without you?

    It's cooler here at night. I actually have blankets on my bed. I have a great big bedroom with old-fashioned oak dressers and big mirrors and a bed that has a huge carved headboard. The whole house is filled with antiques. There's even a bowl and pitcher in my room for me to rinse my hands in the morning. My aunt said that people had those in their rooms in the old days.

because the bathroom might have been an outhouse.

We had such a great dinner last night. Aunt Belinda made mashed potatoes and roasted chicken and homemade bread that was a little sweet. She said the recipe for the bread had come down in the family for generations. But my mom never makes it. I wonder why. I'll have to ask her. In any case, Aunt Belinda gave me a copy of the recipe so maybe I'll try it when I get home.

It's so quiet here. Aunt Belinda doesn't like television so she doesn't have one. And the next house is so far away, I can't even see it. After supper we talked and listened to an opera on the radio. Can you believe that? My parents never play opera music—or really any music at all. All we have is Christmas music during the holidays and children's songs for my brother and Gloria.

Aunt Belinda is so different than my mom. She teaches fourth grade during the day. She never got married, but I think she has a secret. She has a man friend, Jerry, and he lives at the house and takes care of the animals. I don't think even my mom knows that Jerry lives here. He's very nice and has big muscles and I think they make a nice couple. But I'll have to keep this a secret from Mom, just in case Aunt Belinda doesn't want her to know.

Aunt Belinda was so happy that I always wear my locket. I told her how I held tight to it the whole plane ride and that it helped me feel safe.

She asked me if I still had my picture that she put inside it and I said yes. Then she asked if I had put anything else into the locket. I said, "Yes, but it isn't that important to me anymore. It's a silly list in code."

She laughed. "Well, it doesn't matter. Maybe someday you'll put something else in there that's special."

Aunt Belinda always knows exactly what to say to make me feel good, and that's the truth.

Dear Diary,

Today was the most perfect day of my life.
The sky was bright blue with little fluffy clouds.
I slept so long and felt so good when I got up.
I was surprised to find water in the pitcher.
Just for fun I rinsed my hands. I felt like an
old-fashioned girl, which is really different from
what I normally feel like.

When I went downstairs Aunt Belinda had
homemade blueberry muffins on the table.
She offered me milk-coffee to go with them. At
home I never get to have any coffee, except
coffee-flavored ice cream.

After breakfast we walked around the farm.
She showed me all the milking cows. They had
just been milked and were heading out to the
pasture. Some of them had their calves with
them. It was so cute to see them walking side
by side.

She showed me the chickens and the pigs.
The chickens were busy pecking at
their food, and the pigs were busy
rolling in the dirt. And there were
a whole bunch of kittens running

around the barn chasing each other. I felt like I was in a perfect world where all the animals and the people are happy and no one is hurting anyone. It was almost like being in a dream— or in one of the Little House on the Prairie books, though I don't read those anymore either.

Then we went into town. It's a small town with only four blocks and about twelve stores. We parked the car and went in and out of the stores. Aunt Belinda introduced me to everyone she knew.

"This is my favorite niece. I'm so happy she's visiting. She's the best guest!"

I guess I met just about everyone in town.

I felt like the guest of honor at a big ceremony. Everyone asked me questions and told me how pretty I am. It was wonderful.

We ate lunch in the diner. I had a tuna fish sandwich. I took a chance and asked for coffee jello for dessert, but nobody had ever heard of it. So I got coffee-flavored ice cream instead, which was perfectly fine with me.

Then Aunt Belinda took me to a lake and we went swimming and sunbathing. The water in the lake felt so cool and smooth, completely different from the ocean or the pool.

We had dinner at home with Jerry. This time we had scrambled eggs and toast—breakfast for dinner! My aunt was tired and said she didn't feel like making anything more elaborate. But that was okay. I was, too.

We sat out on the porch and watched the sun set and then looked at the stars. We talked a lot. She told me lots of things. I'm too tired to tell you all of them now.

A couple were family secrets. I'll never forget them. Secrets are my favorite thing!

I forgot to tell you that I keep peeling off little strips of my skin. That's because of the sunburn. My mom told me not to do that but I can't help it. It feels so good when I get a really long strip. She said I might peel off too much skin and then I could get an infection. I hope I don't get infected.

I haven't done exercises for my behind since I came out to Minnesota, and I'm eating so much. I hope I'm not gaining weight. But I've been so happy out here that I haven't really thought about it much.

But just in case, I think I'll get down on the floor now and bounce.

Dear Diary,

Here is one of the secrets that Aunt Belinda told me. She has a whole box of old photographs of people who were my relatives. Even though they're all dead now they're still my relatives, of course. She told me that some of the pictures are so strange that she doesn't want me to tell anyone!

She said that our family is a little different from other families. She said that as a schoolteacher she knows that sometimes people make fun of people who are different. And then she said, "You have such nice fair skin, you'll never have to tell."

I really didn't know what she was talking about, but I began to feel shivers running up and down my spine. This sounded like a big secret.

Then she opened the box, really slow like we were having some sort of ceremony. The first picture—you are not going to believe this—was a Native American man wearing a headdress.

Aunt Belinda said, "This is your great-great Uncle Hawthorn." I was in shock.

"What are you talking about?" I said. "We don't have any Native Americans in our family."

"Oh, yes we do," she said. "Uncle Hawthorn married your great-great grandmother's sister, Sara. But it was a terrible secret. Aunt Sara came here with your great-great grandmother when they were little girls. First they lived in Rhode Island and then their father came out to Minnesota with a small group of Jewish families who took up residence and started dairy farms."

Now I was in even more shock. "Jewish families? No one is Jewish in our family. I thought we were Protestant and Catholic."

"No one is Jewish anymore, dear," Aunt Belinda said. "But your Aunt Sara married a Native American man and she was Jewish. The rest of the family never forgave her. It was so sad."

"Do you have a picture of her?" I asked.

"Only this one with their parents when she and your great-great grandmother were little girls."

The picture showed two little girls in frilly white dresses standing next to a man and woman who were dressed in black. The woman

124

had a kerchief on her head and you could only see a little of her hair.

"What happened to my great-great-grandmother?" I asked Aunt Belinda.

"She married a farmer who also had a dairy farm, and they had many children. One of the girls was your great grandmother Miriam."

"Was she Jewish?"

"Oh, no, dear. She was Methodist, just like her husband."

"Did anyone ever hear from Sara again?"

"I don't know. Life is full of mysteries!"

We looked at tons of pictures of all the children and their children. There were portraits done in studios and also pictures taken on the farms where they lived.

A couple of the pictures were of black children. I asked Aunt Belinda who they were.

"One of your great grandmother's brothers married an African American lady he went to elementary school with. The family wasn't happy about that either, but Uncle Nathaniel and his family stayed on a nearby farm and eventually everyone talked to each other again. These are his children."

"Where are they now?"

"I don't know. But it would be easier to find them than Sara's descendents because they have the family last name."

Aunt Belinda sighed. "It's better not to talk about all these mixed-up families. Let's put the box away now."

"Wait, can I take some pictures of those pictures with my phone?"

"Maybe next time." Aunt Belinda said as she put the lid on the box.

"Does my mom know about all this stuff?" I asked her.

"Of course, she's only two years younger than me. We all knew the same things growing up. But when your mother moved away and married your dad, I think she didn't stay interested in the family secrets the way I did. We are so different." she said. And she sounded a bit sad saying it, too.

I asked my aunt if I could tell my mom that she showed me all the pictures.

She said, "Sure. I would never ask you to keep a secret from her. But just remember she may not be as receptive to our ancestry as I am."

I went to sleep that night with my mind in a whirl. I had not really thought about

my ancestors ever. I never dreamed I had
ancestors that were of so many different
mixes. For a long time I couldn't sleep. Wow,
I'm really an amazing mixture and no one
ever bothered to tell me! Why wouldn't Aunt
Belinda let me take some pictures of the
pictures? That bothered me as I finally fell
asleep.

Dear Diary,

Last night I had tons of dreams. In one of the dreams there were all my relatives from long ago. Some of them looked strange and some of them looked nice. There was a big party in some sort of hay field. Except the hay was cut and we had this big space where we were eating hotdogs and corn on the cob and talking. The kids were running around in long skirts and trousers. There were dogs barking and little cats running around, too.

I was wearing a pink dress with sunflowers on it and my hair was much longer than it really is. I had my locket on. I know because I can remember touching it in the dream. I had you with me and I was taking notes in you. I was trying to list who everybody was so I wouldn't forget. Some of the people were Native Americans wearing blankets. Some of the people were African American. There was a lady trying to hand me a necklace that didn't have a locket on it. I think it had a Jewish star like the one Rachel wears to school.

Everyone liked me a lot and wanted me to write down information about them. I couldn't keep up and finally put you away in some sort of big satchel I had, like from Little House on the Prairie. Then the people started to fade away and they kept waving at me and saying, "Don't forget us!"

I wonder if Aunt Belinda will ever tell me any more about them. I hope she does, and I hope she lets me take pictures. I bet she won't say anything else this trip. I just have a feeling I'll have to wait for another time.

Tomorrow I'm going home really early in the morning, so I have to pack now and stop writing to you. I have to get up at 6:00 am to get ready to go to the airport. I can't wait to see everyone. I miss Fifi so much, and I even miss Gloria—but just a little bit.

Dear Diary,

I'm on the airplane now. Something horrible happened last night, maybe when I was packing. I lost my locket again! I couldn't find it anywhere before I went to sleep. I just reached up to touch it as I was getting undressed and it wasn't on me anymore. I don't know if I will ever find it. I don't remember taking it off or anything. All I know is I touched my neck and it wasn't there.

I thought it had fallen into my suitcase, so I emptied everything out and started all over, but it wasn't there. Then I looked all around the room. The floor is wood so it's easy to see something metal on it. There was nothing. I looked in the dresser and on the table and even in the Kleenex box. There was no locket anywhere.

I started to cry and went and found my aunt. She came and helped me look. But it's gone. I might have even lost it in town today when we went to eat lunch in the diner. Or maybe when we were walking in and out of the stores. How will I ever know? All I know is that I don't have it anymore.

I can't believe it's really gone. It means so much to me. I thought Aunt Belinda would be really angry since she gave it to me. But she was nice and said not to worry. She said she will get me another one for my next birthday if I want. But it will never be the same. That one is special. It has my secret code in it. I thought the code was silly and stupid until I lost it. Now I miss it.

I feel awful. It's so strange to be going home without my locket. I keep touching my neck and it's not there.

The airplane is bouncing a lot. I have to stop writing. I feel sick.

Dear Diary,

The first night back home was great.
Everyone came to pick me up at the airport.
Dad, Mom, Grandma, my brother, and Gloria.
We all hugged and cried a little.

When we got home my mom made my
favorite meal. We had T-bone steaks and
baked potatoes. I had my own steak. I loved
every bite. Mom is the best cook.

They wanted me to tell them everything
about my week at Aunt Belinda's. But of
course I didn't. I had to keep a lot of secrets.
I told them all about her house and the farm
and eating out and meeting all her friends
downtown. They thought I was telling them
everything! I guess I'm good at keeping secrets.
Then I went and checked my email but there
wasn't anything. All my friends knew I was
going to be gone anyway. Anyway, I had sent
them lots of selfies from my aunt's farm and
they sent me pictures of themselves, too.

The only terrible thing is not having my
locket. My mom said she would call Aunt
Belinda tomorrow and thank her and ask her

to keep looking for the locket. She told me to
be really careful when I unpack, just in case
it does happen to be in there, tucked into a
corner or something. But I looked, and I'm
pretty sure it's gone forever.

Dear Diary,

I couldn't wait to call Jackie today. She got home from camp at noon, and I was the first person she talked to aside from her parents and brother. I missed her so much. We have to see each other! Mom promised me that I can sleep over at her house tomorrow night. I can't wait.

I'm trying to figure out how much I will tell her about my new secrets. Probably everything. She better tell me everything that happened to her at camp.

I unpacked very carefully today. I shook my suitcase upside down and put my hands everywhere. No locket.

Dear Diary,

Last night I slept over at Jackie's house and we caught up on everything that happened, both at her camp and at Aunt Belinda's house. Jackie had lots of secrets to tell me. One of them really surprised me. She broke up with Larry. I couldn't believe it. I didn't think it would be over so fast. And guess what? Then she went out with Tony! She made out with Tony twice. I felt a little jealous. I haven't even kissed anyone. But I didn't tell her that. I just got all excited and giggled and asked her for all the details. She'll never know that I almost wished she had a rotten time at camp and that I was the one with the kissing stories to tell her.

Then I told her all about my trip to Aunt Belinda's. The real truth. She and you are the only ones who know that there are big secrets in my family. She was fascinated. She said that her family is really boring. Just a whole bunch of Methodists for generations. She said maybe that's why I look a little exotic. I was shocked. I never knew I looked exotic! I asked

Jackie what that means. She said it means I look very interesting and almost a little like I could be a gypsy. She said that men will definitely find me interesting when I'm older, and I'm pretty sure I blushed.

That was such a nice thing for her to say. For a minute I felt really special. Then I remembered my behind and how big it is and I didn't feel so special anymore—just like a bit of a freak.

Jackie also said that maybe when I'm older I'll go on a search and find my extended family. She said lots of people do that. She read about it in the Sunday magazine section of the newspaper once. People find each other and then they all have big family reunions every summer. She said a lot of people look for their relatives online now, and sometimes even find them on Facebook! How cool? And she said I can even get my DNA tested and see what my ethnic percentages are and where around the world my ancestors came from! She is so smart. She knows all this scientific stuff.

Maybe I will search, but only when I'm a lot older. Maybe when I'm eighteen. And then I will do the DNA swab, too.

Dear Diary,

The summer is almost over. My mom and I went to Jack Marono's last night to celebrate my going back to school and starting ninth grade. Guess who was our waiter? The same nice guy and as usual he waited patiently while I was busy telling mom all about Rob (my favorite dinner subject)! I saw him yesterday at the beach. In fact, Jackie, Brian, Rob, and I all stood around and talked for about ten minutes. It was the best day of my life so far. I was wearing my pretty two-piece bathing suit and I just made sure to face Rob so he couldn't see my behind.

We were laughing and joking and shuffling sand with our feet. I got to look at Rob's eyes for ten minutes. I was in heaven. Then they had to leave. Brian's mom was in her car waiting for them. I was bummed but at least we got to hang out for a little bit.

As soon as they drove away Jackie and I collapsed in the sand laughing and hugging each other. We couldn't believe we were really with Brian and Rob, talking and acting like it was so ordinary. The whole time I pretended in my head that I was Rob's girlfriend. It felt really good.

Oh, did I tell you that Jackie still likes Brian? She said she can hardly remember the other two boys from the summer camp. Anyway, how would she get to see anyone from camp now that she's back home? It's better that she like Brian, who is closer and more accessible.

My dream is to go with Rob to the Harvest Dance. It's at the beginning of October. I wonder if my dream will come true? I better keep up with my bouncing exercises!

Dear Diary,

    Some days I am so happy I can't imagine ever being sad again. Today, my first day in ninth grade, was one of those days. First of all, I really liked the way I looked in my new skinny jeans, scoop-neck T-shirt, and ballet flats. In fact, I took a selfie and sent it to my Aunt Belinda and Angela before the bus came. Angela texted me right back with her first day of school selfie. She looks great. Her hair is short and she has a little streak of maroon in it and she is wearing great pale pink lipstick. She is so cool! I felt so good getting her picture and hugs and xxxx's in the text. I finally feel like it is okay to still feel close to her and yet have a best friend here. It can all work out. I also think my mom was right about my moods. My moods are better since I got my period.

    All my teachers are very nice. Jackie is in two of my classes and Betty Ann is in three of them. I'm learning Spanish this year. I'm very excited about that. The only sad thing is that Rob is no longer in my school. He is in the high school. Oh, well. He can still ask me to the Harvest Dance. It is open to all kids from seventh to twelfth grades.

Dear Diary,

School is okay. We have lots of homework already, though. The Harvest Dance is only three weeks away. I'll die if I'm not invited by anyone. And I'll be in heaven if I'm invited by Rob. Jackie and Brian have been talking on the phone every night since we all met at the beach. Brian already asked Jackie to the dance. He thinks Rob will be asking me. When I think about it, my heart starts beating really fast. What if he calls me? What will I say?

Will my dream come true?

Dear Diary,

 My dream has come true! I can hardly believe it. My dad picked up the house phone last night and I heard him say, "Sure, just a minute." Next thing I knew, he was in my room and told me that a guy was on the phone for me. My dad didn't know who it was.

 I could have died. Walking to the phone was the longest ten seconds in my life. What if it was Tom? If he asked me to the dance and I accepted and then Rob asked me, my life would be ruined. I know Tom has a crush on me. I can tell. So the whole walk to the phone I was hoping it wasn't him—anyone but Tom!

 But guess what? It was Rob. Can you believe it? He asked me to the Harvest Dance! Of course I said I would love to go. He said his dad would drive us and they'd come for me at 7:00 p.m. on Friday night. Then he just hung up. I was in a daze.

 Of course I called Jackie right away. Then I told my parents. My mom said I could buy a new dress for the dance. I saw what I want downtown—it's a pale yellow A-line strapless cotton dress. We're not allowed to really dress up. That way no one feels bad if they can't afford new clothes. But I don't mind. I think the shirtdress is cute and I hope Rob thinks so, too.

I don't think I'll sleep tonight. What if this is the beginning of a new relationship for me? What if Rob wants to kiss?

Dear Diary,

Tonight was the dance. It's almost midnight now, but if I don't write to you I will die. It was the best and the worst night in my life. I looked really pretty in my dress. I had curled my hair and pulled it back in a barrette. My dad took lots of pictures of me before I left. And I sent a selfie to Angela. I still have that special spot in my heart for her. I wanted her to see how pretty I looked tonight, and it made me feel like she was just around the corner, not so far away. She sent me a picture back right away of herself babysitting! It was cute to see her with a baby on her lap. I wonder how she held the phone and took the picture without the baby falling off.

It was the best night of my life, because I got to go with Rob. He was very nice to me when he came to pick me up. We had fun at the dance, too. We danced a lot. And he's at least four inches taller than me. He even kissed me good night on the cheek. I guess that counts as my first kiss. And it was magical. I felt so tingly inside after he left.

It was the worst night of my life because guess who his father is? You will never guess. Not in a million years. Give up?

His dad is the waiter at the restaurant! I could have died! His dad was the man who heard all year how much I love Rob! Can you imagine how I felt when I got into the backseat of the car and his dad turned around to say hello to me?

And of course he must have known it would be me. I couldn't tell Rob, though. And I'll never know if Rob knows, which would be mortifying. For all I know his dad pleaded with him to go with me after listening to me all those times, which makes me feel a little nervous. What if Rob only went with me out of pity?

It was so weird. In the car I almost felt like his dad and I had a secret together. I kept sneaking a look at Rob to see if somehow he knew. But he just sat there, smiling and not saying much. I don't know who I am ever going to tell. I guess Jackie—maybe.

Even though we had a nice time I don't feel the same way about Rob now after we spent the evening together. I just keep wondering if he really wanted to ask me. It's

not the same if his dad pushed him to ask
me. But his kiss was so nice. Oh why is this
all so confusing!

Dear Diary,

 I don't know how I feel about Rob. I still think he's cute. But I don't feel the same inside. I feel almost like I lost someone. My mom asked me why I look so tired today. I lied and told her I had a tummy ache coming home from the dance and during the night. She wanted to know all about the dance and told me I probably ate too much candy and too many cupcakes. I really want to tell my mom the truth and get her advice. I just don't know how to do it.

 When I talked to Jackie later, she said I shouldn't feel so bad. She said that Brian told her that Rob really wanted to ask me. I don't know if I believe her. I'm miserable. And how can I trust Brian anyway?

 Also, I still haven't ever been properly kissed. Rob's was only a peck on the cheek. Not hard like Jackie's was this summer. Jackie said it felt amazing to have a real kiss that pushed against her lips kind of hard. She said that she even opened her mouth a little and felt Tony's tongue trying to push into her mouth! She hasn't kissed Brian that way, but she thinks if they go out more they will probably. I'm so jealous. I want to be kissed like that. Of course only by Rob, and only if he means it, not if he is faking.

There are so many things that are just going so wrong. I lost my locket. I feel embarrassed to ever go back to my favorite restaurant. I can't tell my mom what happened. I don't know if Rob really likes me or if he's just trying to be nice. I feel so miserable and so alone and I keep crying. We ran out of Kleenex. I have to use toilet paper to wipe my nose.

I can't stand being me.

Dear Diary,

   The days are going by really slowly. I feel kind of empty sometimes and fine other times. I don't see Rob anymore as he is in high school and takes a different bus. My mom thinks we're going out to the same restaurant next week and that everything is just like normal. My aunt is still looking for my locket. Gloria is trying to stand up. Fifi is kissing my face all the time. I got three A's and two B's on my first big tests. My parents were very proud. We went for an autumn family picnic at the Universal Harmony Church. But inside, I feel kind of empty.

   I did write a new song, though. It goes like this:

Yearnings
I'm crying out.
Who will hear me?
Who will care?
Who will help me get
To a space where I belong?
To a space where I can sing my song?

Where I won't be dismissed.
Or never missed.
I need an answer.
I need some hope.
My yearnings come from so deep inside,
Doesn't anyone hear me cry?
If you do, come here right away.
I don't want to be alone one more day!

But something good did happen. After I wrote the poem I remembered Mom saying we should ask for a family hug whenever we need it. So I went into the kitchen and asked for a family hug. And Mom called everyone in immediately. I was amazed as lots of times she doesn't even seem to really concentrate on what I am saying. And since Grandma was over, that meant all six of us were in a great big family hug. It was wonderful. And guess what? Gloria put out her arms to me when the hug started, so I was holding her as everyone hugged. And we had to stay hugging for at least twenty seconds for the chemistry in our brains to feel happier (as Mom had read), and she made sure the hug lasted a long time. I think it lasted about two minutes, actually.

After that I was in such a good mood! I'm so happy I remembered about the family hugs and asked for one.

Dear Diary,

A miracle has happened. I don't care what the minister said about miracles. I just know miracles happen. When I woke up this morning and I got out of bed, there was my locket on the floor. I don't know how that could be. It wasn't there the night before. I just know it! But it was there now.

My mom said that maybe my unconscious self knew all along where it was and I sleepwalked and found it during the night. She might be right because the light was on when I woke up. It was strange. I never sleepwalked before during the night. But my mom said you don't always know if you have sleepwalked.

I will never know. I just know I was feeling so miserable and now my locket is back and things feel so much better.

But then again, when will I ever feel completely happy again? It's not that I'm miserable. It's that some things hurt so much. Like what happened with Rob. He hasn't really talked to me since the dance and I'm afraid that he probably doesn't like me, or thought

I wasn't pretty enough to be his girlfriend, or was embarrassed by how much I liked him and how his dad knew. Jackie told me he did want to ask me out, but that was weeks ago and nothing has happened since.

At least I have my locket again.

I have to go now. My mom is dropping me off at Jackie's for the afternoon. Jackie said she has more secrets to tell me. I can't wait!

Dear Diary,

    I thought Jackie was going to tell me all her secrets, but instead she told me a secret that Brian just told her. Jackie said that Rob is going to call me this week and ask me to the movies. She said that he feels embarrassed about his dad being the waiter at the restaurant I go to with my mom all those times, but he really does like me. She said I can't tell him ever that Brian told her.

    I feel so relieved I can't even explain it. It is as if I have come alive again. Dear Diary, I am so happy! I can't wait for Rob to call me. Everything feels good again.

Dear Diary,

........Rob just called my cell. He asked me to........
the movies. Jackie and Brian will go with us.
Brian's mom will drive and pick us up. I'm so........
excited. Now I can go on with my life. I can
even go to the restaurant again with my mom.
I'm sure Rob's dad will keep my secret. I'm not........
ready to tell my mom about his identity yet.
Maybe someday, when she will be ready to
tell me some of her secrets about the family........
and why she never told me more about my
ancestors. Maybe then I'll tell her about the
pain I felt when I realized I had been talking........
all year in front of Rob's father about how........
much I loved him. Maybe then we will both be........
ready for sharing our secrets.

........But for now, just being me is good enough,........
as long as being me includes my mom and
dad, Fifi, my brother, Gloria, my grandparents,
my Aunt Belinda, Angela, Jackie, all my........
friends, Rob, my locket, and of course you,........
Dear Diary! Don't worry, you have a lot of
blank pages left, so it will be a long time........
before I have to put you away.

Dear Diary,

Two days until we go to the movies! I can't wait. Life is good. My parents don't fight like they used to. Gloria is crying less at night. I have a new best friend and I'm still in touch with my old best friend. I feel like singing even though I can't remember my old song. It doesn't really matter. Here's what came to me last night:

I'm feeling the strength to go on.
Where is it coming from?
From deep inside me.
How glorious to be!
Happiness fills my being.
I am whole again in my destiny.
Sunshine streams from my new song.
I know in my heart nothing can go wrong!

Discussion Questions for Readers

1. How would you react and feel if you had to move? What would be some of your concerns?
2. Do you keep secrets?
3. Do you share secrets? With whom?
4. How did you feel about the girl deciding not to visit Angela and telling the lie that she had a sore throat?
5. How would you feel if you had to make all new friends?
6. Do you identify with some of the girl's problems? Which ones?
7. How would you feel having a new sister or brother at your age?
8. Is it important to have a best friend? Why?
9. Have you ever wondered about your family background? Does it matter to you who your ancestors were and how they lived?
10. Have you written poems or songs?
11. How could the girl approach her mom to share her feelings and concerns more honestly?

12. What are some of the ways we can handle our feelings when we're afraid to be up front and feel we have to keep a secret?

13. Is it always smart to keep a secret? When is it not?

14. What do you see happening to the girl in school the rest of her school year? The book ends in mid-October of the ninth grade.

15. What do you think are the most important issues the girl should try to handle this year?

16. What would you like to name her? Why?

17. Have you worried about how you look? Felt too fat? What do you think about how the girl handles her feelings about her body?

18. What would you like to happen to the girl in the next book? What are some of the possibilities? I'd love to hear from you with your ideas. You can write to me at drbarbara@enchantedself.com.

These questions are to get you started. Feel free to use the next couple of pages to answer the above, to write other personal feelings and thoughts, or to write your own song.

About the Author

Dr. Barbara Becker Holstein, nationally known Positive Psychologist, is the creator of The Enchanted Self,® a systematic way of helping bring more joy, meaning, and purpose into our lives.

Dr. Holstein has been a school psychologist for over twenty-five years. She also taught first and second grades. She is in private practice as a psychologist, with her husband, Dr. Russell M. Holstein, in Long Branch, New Jersey.

You can find Dr. Holstein on the web at www.enchantedself.com, at *The Truth* blog at www.thetruthforgirls.com, on Facebook at www.facebook.com/thetruthforgirls, and you can write to her at drbarbara@enchantedself.com.